CANCEL & TEAR

For you

FOR YOU

"And with thy bloody and invisible hand

Cancel and tear to pieces that great bond"

- Hamlet Act: III, Scene II

I. DAWN - TOGETHER

Carmine stands half-naked before first light, out
Leaning right above the untroubled turnpike,
Gazing sternly into the sunlight splitting,
Hewn by the buildings,

Into daylight. Julia calls from bed, still
Lounging. Carmine hears but doesn't answer. Clambers
Through the window after a moment passes.
"Omelet with cheese?" she

Asks, solicits. "Really, no time for breakfast,"
Zips his pants and buttons his shirt. The morning
Clamor's nearby. Julia sighs. A neighbor
Screams at her husband.

Roadways grow progressively louder. Carmine
Hears a swallow chirruping over traffic.
Now she comes, embraces him tightly, kisses
Softly his forehead.

Sometimes, through the window, a breeze will enter
Chilling both their legs. With the wind the city's
Fetor rises. Turning towards the mirror,
Used to the stench now,

Carmine watches Julia dress for work. He
Saunters over checking his hair. He strokes her
Cheek. He sees his hand is transparent, palm and
Fingers are vanished.

Carmine's heart aches. Julia hears it pounding
Nearly through his chest and she turns to him. He
Says, "I'm late for work!" and intensely kisses
Julia. "Love you!".

II. MORNING – APART

Head down, hands held deep in his pockets, hiding,
Rays of dim municipal light fluoresce on
Carmine, grimly hastening on beneath the
Boulevard's jungle

A startling vibration in his jacket pocket.
A message on his phone.

The people dashing past look all
In a ravenous hunger to arrive.
He's not so anxious,

Though his cellphone tells him,
"Urgent! Photos needed for breaking news…".
Carmine's been disappearing for months now.

So he doesn't respond.
Instead, he slips into an alleyway,
A shortcut to no place in particular.

He whispers to himself aloud,
"What use is work when you're dying?"

He skips the subway and wanders
Through a forlorn district
Thinking, "What will she do
Once I've disappeared completely?"

In an alley where he's never been,
Carmine pictures a familiar scene
That takes him back to the desert war.

He remembers a photograph he took
Early in the crusade, his first days -
A kneeling woman shot, holding a boy.

Maybe she was praying. Maybe both were praying.
What good did that do them?

Carmine wondered then, "Who can ever know?"

He thought about this for weeks then,
Asking himself, "What good does this do us?"

He progressed, "What happens when you die?"

He reaches an intersection, "Can anyone be saved?

He reaches an understanding, "The living can't be saved"

This is when it first occurred,
Here and there disappearances.

Carmine began to photo death as art:
A soldier killed where he stood -
Backed into a corner, but never fallen;

A rebel suicide bomber shot
Only just before detonation.

In those times, death became art -
An end in itself.

Carmine was invisible for a week once.

They thought he was dead
Or captured. He had gone walking the streets
Watching people as they died.

Shortly after this he was discharged,
A kind of dying.

The vision of the woman makes him think,
"Now I understand. They were already dead."

Carmine's wandered clear across the city,
Come back down to earth from his impressions.

He's somewhere near his old digs now,
A few blocks down from the flat he rented long
Before the war. Before Julia. Before death.

He sees someone he knows, a high school friend
Still living in this old hood. Carmine turns to go,
Avoid the encounter. He thinks, "Why am I afraid?"

His old pal calls to him from across the road,
Carmine turns and suddenly vanishes in his place.

He doesn't look back. He thinks of Julia.
He is at peace with her and remembers
Their very first times together, after the war.

He was walking the city streets at night,
Lonesome. Wandering in search of death,

Lurking out on the scaffolding of old mens'
Apartments and hospital wards and ghettos
Where junkies died without realizing,
Thinking death was just another high.

Carmine wandered in these places then
In search of beauty, in search of death.

Once, on a cold night, he strolled near the river
To watch the lights reflect off the water
Beyond the beaten path.

Julia was there, in a summer skirt and sandals,
Shivering, crying quietly.

Carmine was struck. A lightening bolt. A flash.

He'd been invisible the entire evening.
When he went to her she looked up in surprise.

Julia cured him.

For months now he has gone without a day
Out of body wandering the city streets.
Death has gone.

Julia is life. There is no more, no need for more.

He wonders, "Why today? What has happened now,
That all of this returned?"

He doesn't understand.
He appears again, flesh and all
Where he's supposed to be.

III. NOON - TOGETHER

Sometimes, Fridays mostly, but never when its
Raining, Carmine takes his beloved strolling
Near the water, picnicking under shady
Trees, just the same as

When he started dating her months ago. She
Waits beneath a sycamore, first presage that
Summer's ending drifts to the ground around her.
Carmine approaches,

Slightly late and breathing severely, saying,
"Love, I'm sorry. Hurried as fast as traffic
Granted." "Well, its fine. I enjoy the park," she
Says. And so Carmine

Sits beside her. Julia asks how work was.
"Work was fine," he says. This without a glance at
Her. Afraid, confused, he observes a leaf that's
Dying, descending;

Picks a tuft of grass and examines each small
Spear directly. Julia comes, caresses
Carmine's arm, remarking, "Like satin. Feather
Soft." And she leans in

Pursing lips and kissing the edge of Carmine's
Mouth. He shuts his eyes and imagines life will
Never better all the desires fulfilled in
Only this moment.

Carmine runs his fingers through her exquisite
Hair to comfort Julia, who is lying
Calmly in his arms. She looks up for Carmine's
Face, which has vanished.

IV. AFTERNOON - APART

And his eyes and his arms and his body
They've vanished too.
But the feel of him remains.

Julia asks herself, "Is this my imagination?"
Mind rushing, face glowing red;
A specter of fear is creeping, quickly.

She starts to slip from his embrace.
She calls out, "Where are you Carmine?
Please don't play these games with me!"

He calls back, "I'm right in front of you."

She thinks the leaves are falling faster now
And feels like autumn is on the very cusp.
She doesn't know what to think.

She can't see Carmine crawling closer
But feels his hand rest on her hand.
Julia jumps up, gasps; confused.

Again, she feels his hand on hers
But can only see the imprint of his feet
Weighing down the grass beneath him.

Carmine completely disappears
Into the single tear spilling
From the seas in Julia's eyes.

People pass along staring at her talking to no one,
Pointing her out to their companions;
Wondering, for all to hear, "What's wrong with her?"

Some assume the city just turns everyone insane.
Some wonder aloud, "Why is she crying?"

One man feels brave enough to approach her
And ask if she needs assistance.

Carmine's presence is faded from the atmosphere
And Julia turns to the man in tears then turns away,
Running fast in the opposite direction.

Julia calmly walks into the flow of traffic.

The man in the large blue SUV curses her
As he abruptly swerves to prevent something tragic.
Julia doesn't comprehend; her mind's gone elsewhere.

She makes it to the other side, as if by magic,
Bumping into people as she passes them.
They wince at her and murmur to themselves.

Her arms are wrapped around her. She's shivering
Not for lack of warmth, but for lack of Carmine's
Hand around her waist as she walks through the city.

Julia's mind races. Among the thoughts crossing are,
"Carmine was all of my possibilities. Everything,"
And a constant screaming, "Carmine, where are you?"

They'd dreamed of leaving the city together.
A house on a lake, the leaves changing color -
Yellow and red - and the last birds of summer
Warbling in the window they would have.

They'd wanted to get married on the island,
Knee deep in the water, and rows of floating candles
Lighting the passageway out to their ocean.

Just the other day they'd planned a trip
To a port city far up in the nether regions,
Where the winds are chilly even in the summer.

Julia screams to herself, "Carmine where are you?"
While she drifts further from the world.

She's come to their residence
That can no longer be called their home.
Now its just another flat, abandoned in the city.
Filled, not with people, but increasingly distant memories.

Julia asks herself as she sulks up the stairs heavily,
"What's going on? Why is this going on? Carmine!
How long has this been going on!"

Something in her spirit drags her up the stairs,
A brisk walk then running then mad dashing,
Sprinting up seven flights at an unsafe speed.

Julia has drifted from of the world, completely.

She fights through the heavy door
To their former apartment.

She drags past a lounge chair
And sinks to the balcony
Expecting to find Carmine waiting.

She searches in that space's four corners,
Finding nothing.

She screams out over the city,
To the city, "Carmine, where are you!"

Crying out, wailing, weeping,
Julia falls to her knees,
Head bowed, clutching the terrace's metal bars,
Mourning, "Carmine, Carmine where are you?"

V. SUNSET - TOGETHER

Carmine asks her, "Praying to which god?" kneeling
Down beside her, placing his limpid hand so
Softly on her. Julia turns to Carmine
Noticing only

Teardrops streaming down, silhouetting where his
Face would be. She kisses him where his eyes would
Be then stares at Carmine, reflecting on the
Tears, now profusely

Running down their faces. She takes his hand and
Leads them through the flat to the bathroom, stopping
There. She feels alongside the hidden line of
Carmine's soft lips. She

Kisses Carmine. Julia turns the shower
On, undresses clothes that aren't even there then
Feels his veiled and tender caresses slowly
Peeling away the

Clothes from every slant of her supple body.
Once below the sprinkling shower, water
Droplets outline Carmine's physique so clearly
Julia makes out

Every contour, kisses and strokes the entire
Scope of Carmine's body. Embracing under
Water, made of only an outline, Carmine
Kisses her forehead

Such that neither lover can hear the traffic
Rushing, fuming, deafening further down than
Even sunlight goes in this dark of nightfall
Covering all things.